It's the coolest school in space!

Young Teggs Stegosaur is a pupil at
Astrosaurs ACADEMY – where dinosaurs
train to be space-exploring **Astrosaurs**.
With his best friends Blink and Dutch
beside him, amazing adventures and
far-out fun are never far away!

Collect all the **Astrosaurs ACADEMY**
books. Free collector cards in every
one for you to swap with your friends.

For more astro-fun visit the website
www.astrosaursacademy.co.uk

Read all the adventures of Teggs, Blink and Dutch!

DESTINATION: DANGER!
CONTEST CARNAGE!
TERROR UNDERGROUND!

Read Teggs's adventures as a real ASTROSAUR!

RIDDLE OF THE RAPTORS
THE HATCHING HORROR
THE SEAS OF DOOM
THE MIND-SWAP MENACE
THE SKIES OF FEAR
THE SPACE GHOSTS
DAY OF THE DINO-DROIDS
THE TERROR-BIRD TRAP
THE PLANET OF PERIL
TEETH OF THE T. REX
specially published for World Book Day
THE STAR PIRATES
THE CLAWS OF CHRISTMAS
THE SUN-SNATCHERS
REVENGE OF THE FANG

Find out more at www.astrosaurs.co.uk

TERROR UNDERGROUND!

Illustrated by Woody Fox

RED FOX

TERROR UNDERGROUND!
A RED FOX BOOK 978 1 862 30557 1

First published in Great Britain by Red Fox,
an imprint of Random House Children's Books
A Random House Group Company

This edition published 2008

1 3 5 7 9 10 8 6 4 2

The Random House Group Limited supports the Forest Stewardship
Council (FSC), the leading international forest certification
organization. All our titles that are printed on Greenpeace-approved
FSC-certified paper carry the FSC logo. Our paper procurement policy
can be found at www.rbooks.co.uk/environment.

Mixed Sources
Product group from well-managed
forests and other controlled sources
www.fsc.org Cert no. TT-COC-2139
© 1996 Forest Stewardship Council
FSC

Set in16/20pt Bembo Schoolbook by
Falcon Oast Graphic Art Ltd

Red Fox Books are published by Random House Children's Books,
61–63 Uxbridge Road, London W5 5SA

www.**kids**at**randomhouse**.co.uk
www.**rbooks**.co.uk

Addresses for companies within The Random House Group Limited can
be found at: www.randomhouse.co.uk/offices.htm

THE RANDOM HOUSE GROUP Limited Reg. No. 954009

A CIP catalogue record for this book is available from
the British Library.

Printed in the UK by CPI Bookmarque, Croydon, CR0 4TD

For Natalie Dallaire,
black widow battler

WELCOME TO THE COOLEST SCHOOL IN SPACE . . .

Most people think that dinosaurs are extinct. Most people believe that these weird and wondrous reptiles were wiped out when a massive space rock smashed into the Earth, 65 million years ago.

HA! What do *they* know? The dinosaurs were way cleverer than anyone thought . . .

This is what *really* happened: they saw that big lump of space rock coming, and when it became clear that dino-life could not survive such a terrible crash, the dinosaurs all took off in huge, dung-powered spaceships before the rock hit. They set their sights on the stars and left the Earth, never to return . . .

Now, 65 million years later, both plant-eaters and meat-eaters have built massive empires in space. But the carnivores are never happy unless  they're causing trouble. That's why the Dinosaur Space Service needs herbivore heroes to defend the Vegetarian Sector. Such heroes have a special name. They are called ASTROSAURS.

But you can't change from a dinosaur to an astrosaur overnight. It takes years of training on the special planet of Astro Prime in a *very* special place . . . the Astrosaurs Academy! It's a sensational

space school where
manic missions
and incredible
adventures are
the only
subjects! The
academy's doors
are always open,
but only to the
bravest, boldest
dinosaurs . . .

And to YOU!

*NOTE: One of the most famous astrosaurs of
all is Captain Teggs Stegosaur. This
staggering stegosaurus is the star of many
stories . . . But before he became a spaceship
captain, he was a cadet at Astrosaurs
Academy. These are the adventures of the
young Teggs and his friends — adventures
that made him the dinosaur he is today!*

Talking Dinosaur!

How to say the prehistoric names in
TERROR UNDERGROUND!

STEGOSAUR – *STEG-oh-SORE*

DIPLODOCUS – *di-PLOH-de-kus*

DICERATOPS – *dye-SERRA-tops*

ANKYLOSAUR – *an-KILE-oh-SORE*

AMMOSAURUS – *AM-oh-SORE-us*

TOROSAURUS – *TOR-oh-SORE-us*

RAPTOR – *RAP-tor*

The cadets

THE DARING DINOS

Teggs   Dutch   Blink

DAMONA'S DARLINGS

Damona   Netta   Splatt

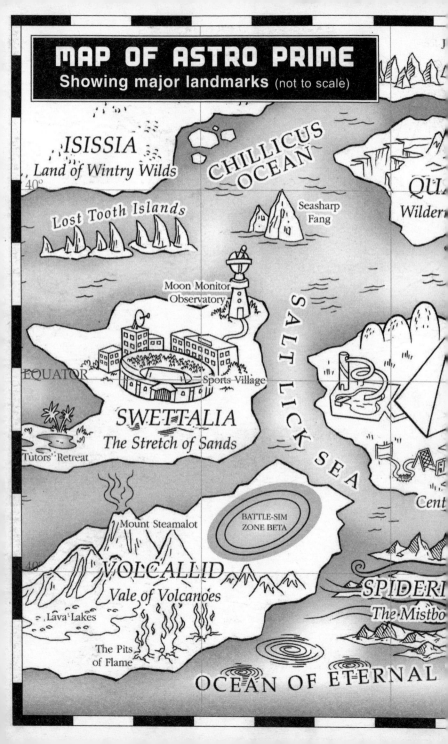

Chapter One

PERIL IN THE SKY

With a supersonic roar, a dozen astro-
jets shot through the bright blue skies of
Astro Prime. They loop-the-looped and
whizzed past each other at incredible
speed . . .

"Wow, that is *totally* awesome!" Standing in a snowy field far below, Teggs Stegosaur clapped as the spacecraft zoomed overhead. So did his fellow classmates.

They were all cadets at Astrosaurs Academy, where ordinary dinosaurs trained to be dynamic space-explorers. Usually they had their lessons in a warm, cosy classroom. But today, wrapped up in thermal suits, they had travelled to the frozen north pole of the planet for a special flying demonstration . . .

"Look at those astro-jets go!" squawked Blink Fingawing. He was a bright yellow dino-bird with glasses perched on his inquisitive beak. "Just think – later today we get to ride in one."

2

"I can't wait," said Dutch Delaney, a dark green diplodocus. He hugged himself with his long tail. "It'll be warmer for a start! Why do they have to hold this big flying show somewhere so cold, anyway?"

"You dino-dimwit!" scoffed a pretty red diceratops, walking over. "Don't you know your history?"

"Brace yourself, guys." Teggs winced. "Here comes Damona Furst – the number one pain at Astrosaurs Academy!"

"Number one *star*, you mean." Damona stuck out her tongue. "Sixty years ago, the final battle of Raptor War Ten was fought right here over Isissia, the coldest continent on  Astro Prime. The rotten old raptors lost."

"We know," said Blink. "Every year, the astrosaurs who fought that battle return to Astro Prime to celebrate their victory."

"And tomorrow they will all arrive for a big feast and a super-cool astro-jet display!" said Teggs happily, watching the jets come in to land.

"What you might *not* know," said Damona smugly, "is that Grand Marshal Gronko, my grandad, fought in the battle. Last summer he taught me his top flying tips. He says I'm a cool pilot."

"A *fool* pilot more like!" Dutch retorted, and Damona elbowed him in the ribs.

"Right, you lot!" Commander Gruff, the grizzled green head teacher at Astrosaurs Academy, stared round at his cadets, an unripe banana clamped in his mouth like a cigar. "You've seen our top pilots in action. Now, get into your teams and choose a jet – it's time for your first test flights!"

Teggs grinned at Blink and Dutch and held out his hand. "I know our team is called the Daring Dinos . . . but do we dare to fly an astro-jet?"

Blink and Dutch put their hands on top of his. "WE DARE!" the three friends shouted together, before racing towards the launch pads.

Just behind them, Damona had gathered her own team-mates – a cheeky ankylosaur named Netta, and super-speedy Splatt, the racing reptile. Splatt whizzed ahead of everyone to claim the newest, shiniest astro-jet for his team, Damona's Darlings. Damona and Netta high-fived him and looked

very pleased with themselves.

The Daring Dinos shrugged and grabbed themselves a slightly scorched and dented astro-jet.

"For the next hour, these jets will fly you around the practice zone on autopilot while you get used to the controls," Gruff told the cadets. "Colonel Erick, my top flight instructor, will go up with each team in turn to give special training."

Erick – a blue ammosaurus – stepped

out from
behind one
of Gruff's
giant legs and
smiled. "Come
on then, group,"
he bellowed. "Jump
on board!"

The cadets
crowded eagerly
into their astro-
jets. Teggs
followed Dutch and Blink inside, almost
bursting with excitement. He had
always dreamed of flying spaceships!
Then he glanced back and gulped.

Colonel Erick was striding up behind
him!

"I'll fly with your team first, Teggs,"
Erick announced. "My hobby is
tinkering with old spaceships."

"That's a cool hobby!" Teggs declared.

Erick grinned and strode aboard.

"Commander Gruff says I can do up this one after the display. C'mon, cadet. Let's check out this crate!"

Teggs followed him into the large computerized cockpit. Dutch and Blink were arguing over who got to start up the engines. Noticing Erick, they blushed and fell silent.

"All set to take off on autopilot, sir," said Blink sheepishly.

"If you mean we're ready to rock 'n' roll, Blink, just say so!" Erick yanked down on the take-off lever, and the Daring Dinos whooped with delight as the astro-jet roared upwards. "I'll just take us out of the practice zone and into the open skies . . ."

The minutes passed like seconds. Blink and Dutch watched in awe as Erick's claws flicked smoothly over the controls,  but Teggs couldn't help staring at the incredible view through the cockpit window. The icy wastelands far below seemed to stretch on for ever, glittering in the sunlight. "Wow," he breathed.

"We're now flying at a height of twenty thousand metres," said Erick, turning to Dutch. "Would you like to take us even higher?"

Dutch jumped up and grinned. "You know it, dude – um, sir!"

But suddenly, Blink noticed something on one of the computer screens.

"Colonel Erick?" he twittered. "I think another craft is heading our way."

Erick frowned. "The other cadets' astro-jets are set to autopilot. They've been programmed not to fly out of the practice zone."

"I think this one has forgotten its programming!" Teggs gulped as a shiny ship came zigzagging wildly towards them at high speed. "Colonel, I think it's going to—"

KA-BOOOOOOM!

With a senses-shattering explosion,
the two astro-jets collided! Teggs was
hurled to the floor and the cockpit
erupted in smoke and flames.

"The controls have burned out." Erick
gasped as the craft went into a
screaming nose dive. "Grab hold of
something, cadets – we're going to
crash!"

Chapter Two

DISASTER IN THE DARK

The Daring Dinos'
astro-jet plummeted
from the sky faster
than a speeding
meteor. Through the
window they saw
the vast blank sheets
of snow and ice
rushing up to meet
them.

Terrified, Teggs
barely had time to
draw a breath before
it was punched from
his lungs by the force

of an incredible crash-landing. The
sound of splintering ice and twisting
metal almost blew his ears off. All the
lights went out. The crumpled craft was
hurled about like a tin can in a
hurricane, sending the cadets flying
between floor, walls and ceiling . . .

Finally, the astro-jet screeched and
skidded to a stop. Dutch tripped over
Teggs's head, and Blink bashed into
his tail. For several minutes they lay
still, panting for breath in the freezing
darkness. Then Teggs got up. He felt
bruised all over but
nothing seemed to
be broken.

"Colonel Erick?" Teggs called into the darkness. There was no reply.

"Ow! I – I can't move my left wing," Blink twittered. "Dutch, are you sitting on it?"

Dutch groaned. "I'll let you know when I find my butt!"

"Hold still, you two. I'll try to find the emergency lights . . ." Groping his way to the smoking controls, Teggs flicked a few switches and got lucky. A single bulb shone thin light into the ruined control room. Now Teggs could see Erick sprawled on the floor, snoring, with a big lump on his head.

15

"He's knocked out cold," Teggs
reported, crouching beside him. "But I
think he'll be all right."

Suddenly, they heard a loud
scrabbling sound just outside. "Is
everyone OK?" came a familiar voice.

"Damona!" Teggs gasped. "Then it
was *your* astro-jet that collided with us!"

"I'm sorry. We couldn't help it."
Damona came inside, scuffed and
scratched, clutching a first aid kit. "Our

autopilot stopped working, and we . . . we . . ." Her eyes filled with tears. "We went out of control and hit you."

Dutch glared at her. "So much for your top pilot skills!"

"There was nothing I could do," Damona insisted, wiping her eyes. "And now both jets have crash-landed in a deep crack in the ice."

Blink frowned and straightened his glasses. "Are Splatt and Netta OK?"

"They're outside setting up a signal flare so Gruff will know where to find us." Damona opened her first aid kit. "Now, I'd better take a look at beak-brain's dodgy wing . . ."

"We need a stretcher for Colonel Erick, too," Dutch added. "I'll try to knock one together."

"Good idea," said Teggs. "I'll see how the others are getting along."

He stepped outside into a kind of icy cave. The walls sparkled in the light of an emergency lantern. Scrawny Splatt was unpacking the signal flare, which looked like a small rocket. Netta was using her powerful tail to whack a hole in the ground for the rocket to stand in.

Then Teggs looked up – and gasped. The battered jets were stuck at the bottom of a staggeringly tall ice mountain. All he could see of the sky was a crack of blue maybe a mile above. "We really *are* a long way down," he muttered.

"Hey, Teggs!" cried Splatt, his voice echoing crazily off the icy walls. "Is everyone OK?"

Teggs shushed him quickly. "Just about," he hissed. "But don't speak too loudly. We've smashed through thousands of tons of snow and ice, remember – the whole area will be very fragile. You could bring an avalanche down on top of us!"

Splatt pretended to zip up his mouth, and Teggs turned to Netta. "Is the flare ready to launch?"

Netta nodded. "Nearly. It was a bit damaged in the crash but—"

Suddenly, a bloodcurdling scream rang out, and Teggs and Netta jumped in the air. It was Splatt!

"I saw something move!" he gabbled, pointing past Damona's crashed jet towards a large dark hole in the cave wall. "Something huge and hairy and horrible, down that tunnel!"

"Stop shouting," Teggs urged him. But already, the ground was trembling under his feet, and the massive ice mountain above had started to shake. "Uh-oh!"

"Too late!" Netta shrieked as lumps of snow came tumbling down on them. "It's an avalaaaaaaaanche!"

Dutch and Damona rushed from the ruined astro-jet carrying Colonel Erick on a stretcher they'd cobbled together from two floor panels and a broken seatbelt. Blink hopped hurriedly after them with one wing strapped up. The flurries of ice and rock fell on them like hard rain. A low, rumbling roar was building and echoing all around.

"If this keeps up we'll be squashed flat!" Blink squawked.

Teggs nodded. "We must shelter in that tunnel."

"But that's where I saw the horrible hairy thing!" Splatt protested.

"Oh, no!" wailed Netta as a huge boulder flattened the signal flare. "Now we can't get help!"

Damona dragged Blink aside as another rock missed him by millimetres. "That tunnel's our only chance. Come on!"

Desperately, the astrosaur cadets raced into the tunnel carrying their injured instructor. Looking back, they saw tons and tons of falling snow and ice swamp their landing site, burying the jets and blotting out the distant crack of daylight high above. Even the mouth of the tunnel was soon blocked by frozen boulders. Teggs eyed the roof worriedly and hoped it wouldn't fall in on them.

Finally, the crashing stopped. All was dark and eerily silent. Then Damona flicked on a torch. The beam of white light showed nothing but ice and shadow – and the cadets' own frightened faces.

"Nice going, Splatt," said Dutch. "Now we're trapped down here."

"We'll never get out," whispered Splatt, wide-eyed. "*Never!*"

Chapter Three

MONSTER!

Splatt's gloomy words hung in the freezing air.

"Come on, guys," said Teggs, forcing a smile. "If we give up before we start, we really *won't* get out."

"Teggs is right." Damona shone her torch into the shadows. "Let's see where this passageway leads."

"I've read about the underground ice tunnels of Isissia," Blink whispered.

"There's meant to be millions of them winding beneath the surface for miles and miles . . ."

Dutch shrugged. "If there's that many tunnels, one of them *must* lead to the surface, right?" He stooped to pick up the stretcher, where Colonel Erick was still asleep. "Let's move, dudes."

"What about that *thing* Splatt saw in here?" said Netta nervously. "It might be waiting further down the passage."

Splatt nodded. "I only glimpsed it, but . . ." He lowered his voice to a throaty whisper. "It looked like a giant spider – bigger than all of us put together!"

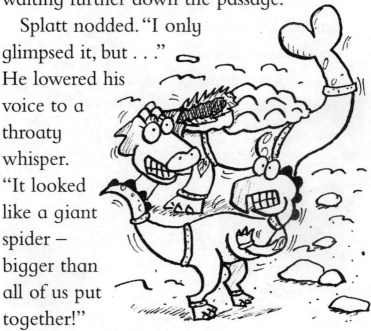

Teggs felt a sharp shiver go through him.

"You must have imagined it, Splatt," said Blink. "There *are* no giant spiders on Astro Prime. And even tiny ones couldn't survive somewhere as cold as this."

"Well, in that case, beak-face," said Damona slowly, "what made *this*?"

Teggs and the others turned to find that Damona had ventured a little way along the tunnel. And something up ahead was glinting in the light of her torch beam.

It looked like an enormous spider web – and it was completely blocking their way!

"Who's afraid of a mouldy old cobweb?" Dutch marched up to it and swiped it with his tail. But the web didn't break, and his tail almost got stuck in it!

Teggs picked up a small boulder from the ground and hurled that at the cobweb instead. But it caught in the sticky strands like an oversized fly.

Netta frowned. "That is one tough web."

"And the spider who spun it must be even tougher!" squeaked Splatt.

"There's another tunnel leading off here," Damona reported, shining her torch to the left of the giant web.

"Then let's take a look," said Teggs.

Dutch and Splatt hefted the stretcher and followed Teggs and Damona cautiously into the dark tunnel, Blink and Netta close behind. The ground was slippery, and the walls were rough. Other passages led off from the tunnel, but more spider webs blocked the entrances.

Almost as if we were being steered somewhere, thought Teggs worriedly.

Round the next corner, the tunnel opened up into another icy cavern. Teggs gasped, and so did Damona.

Part of an enormous spaceship was sticking out of a giant snowdrift in front of them!

Damona stared. "Where did *that* come from?"

"I don't know," said Teggs. He could just make out a set of double doors, blurred by thick layers of ice. "But if it's got a working communicator, perhaps we can get a message to Commander Gruff."

"I hope so!" Damona turned back to Blink, Dutch, Splatt and Netta. "Guys, look what we've—*EEEEK!*"

Teggs spun round and got the shock of his life. Two large, glowing red eyes were watching them all from the darkness!

Splatt, Blink and Netta yelled in
alarm and everyone sprinted out of the
tunnel.

"Quick!" cried Teggs. "Shelter inside
the spaceship."

"We can't," panted Damona, shining
her torch over the mysterious craft.
"The doors are completely iced up!"

"Not for much longer," Netta
growled. She pounded the ice with her
powerful tail. Teggs helped her, while
Splatt, Dutch and Damona hurled rocks
and snowballs at the mouth of the
tunnel, hoping to drive the red-eyed
monster away.

"We're through!" Teggs cheered as the last of the ice shattered.

Still chucking snowballs, Dutch whacked the entry control with his tail. But nothing happened. "There's no power," he groaned. "The doors still won't open—"

"*The monster's coming!*" cried Splatt.

Teggs turned to see the hairy tips of two colossal creepy-crawly legs emerging from the mouth of the tunnel . . .

Chapter Four

AN ICE SURPRISE

The cadets stared in horror as a hideous
giant spider slowly crept out of the
passage. Its legs were like furry tree trunks
and its mouth was a dark twitching hole
crammed full of toothy spikes.

The spider watched them, red eyes
glinting in the
torchlight . . .

At that
precise moment,
Colonel Erick
woke up. "Oh,
my head!" he
groaned, still
dazed.

"Glad you're feeling better, sir," said Teggs, yanking him to his feet. "We need your transport!" The stegosaurus started stacking the empty stretcher with chunks of ice and rock. "Splatt, Blink, look after the colonel. The rest of you, help me here!"

Dutch picked up a big lump of ice and frowned. "What are we doing, dude?"

"You'll see," said Teggs, as Netta and Damona helped him pile up the stretcher with frozen rocks. "If we all push together . . ."

The eight-legged horror was still watching them from the tunnel. It tensed its quivering legs, as if about to leap forward.

"Quick!" cried Teggs. He started pushing the stretcher like it was an enormous toboggan. Damona, Dutch and Netta joined him, shoving with all their strength. The makeshift sledge sped across the slippery ground and crashed

into the mouth of the tunnel. The spider vanished from view as the huge load of snow and ice sealed up the entrance.

"You did it!" cheered Blink behind them.

"We sure did," said Dutch, giving Teggs a high-five while Netta and Damona shared a hug.

"Eh?" Blink turned, saw what had happened and grinned. "Wow, well done, guys! But I was actually talking to Colonel Erick — he's managed to open the doors *and* get the ship's power systems working again."

Erick was standing on Splatt's shoulders, fiddling with some wires in a hatch above the entrance. "All done!" he said, jumping down. "I've switched extra energy  to the heaters, so the ship should thaw out in no time. Told you I love tinkering with old spaceships . . ."

"*I* love being able to hide inside one of them," said Teggs as he and the others followed Erick inside. "Because I doubt our hairy friend will stay stuck in that tunnel for long . . ."

The spaceship was dimly lit but already wonderfully warm. The floors were wet with melting ice dripping from the walls and ceiling. Teggs shut the doors and locked them so the spider couldn't get in. He had expected Erick to be angry and anxious now he knew about their predicament. But instead the flight instructor seemed excited.

"Damona, I'm almost glad you crashed that astro-jet. If you hadn't we would never have found such an incredible piece of history." Erick shook his head in amazement. "We are standing inside a DSS Mega-jet Alpha. They're enormous ships, at least a century old. I've only ever seen a model of one in a museum. We must try and get it back to the surface so it can be restored . . ."

"Then this is an astrosaur spaceship, sir?" asked Splatt.

Erick nodded. "The green stripes on the wall tell us it's a science-ship – like a space lab for interplanetary experiments. Very few were made and they were all top secret."

"Wow," said Dutch. "Do you think it crashed here during Raptor War Ten?"

"I don't know," Erick admitted. "But the ice should have kept the ship's systems

perfectly preserved.
With luck, we
can send an
SOS from
the control
room."

He frowned. "Only thing is, there are three levels on this ship, and I'm not sure where the control room is."

"We could split into groups and search," Teggs suggested.

Damona nodded. "And meet back here in twenty minutes."

"Good plan, cadets," said Erick. "I'll take Blink and Splatt and search Level Three."

"Netta, you come with me," said Damona, ushering her through the door. "I bet we find the control room on Level One."

"Bet you don't!" Dutch called after them. "Come on, Teggs, we'll show those girls . . ."

The groups went their separate ways through the silent, shadowy ship.

Teggs and Dutch climbed the steps to Level Two. The ship was almost *too* warm now, but the heating had melted all the ice.

"I just had a thought," said Teggs. "What happened to the crew?"

Dutch pulled a face. "They might be skeletons or something . . ." He shuddered. "Maybe we *should* let the girls find the control room!"

"Too late," said Teggs, his heart thumping as he opened another door. "I think this is it!"

The room beyond was big and circular, full of blinking lights and clunky, old-fashioned controls. Dominating the room was a large chair. With a sudden start, Teggs saw there was an equally large grey figure slumped in it, wearing astrosaur uniform!

Dutch gulped. "That must be the captain."

Cautiously, Teggs splashed across the floor to get a closer look. "She's a torosaurus," he whispered, eyeing the three horns and large head-frill. "She's been frozen in the ice . . . and she's still breathing!"

"No way!" said Dutch.

"She is!" Teggs marvelled. "The ice must have kept *her* preserved for all these years, as well as the ship's controls . . ."

Suddenly, Damona and Netta appeared in the doorway. They looked upset.

"Don't sulk because we found this place first, dudes," said Dutch. "Just get in here. You won't believe what we've found . . ."

"You won't believe what *we've* found either," said Damona grimly, as she and Netta were shoved forward.

Teggs and Dutch stared, astounded.

Behind the girls, holding old-fashioned
ray-guns and baring their sharp yellow
teeth, were two revolting, wrinkly, meat-
eating dinosaurs in blood-red
battle-armour . . .

Raptors!

Chapter Five

MEMORY MYSTERY

"This must be a bad dream," cried
Dutch. "First we find giant spiders and a
spooky frozen torosaurus – now a pair
of raptors!"

"They were waiting in a big lab on
Level One." Netta glared at their raptor
captors, and Teggs noticed a sparkling
gold band on her
wrist. "I'd just
found a really
cool bracelet
lying on the
table when they
jumped out and
got us!"

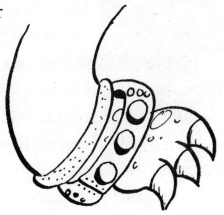

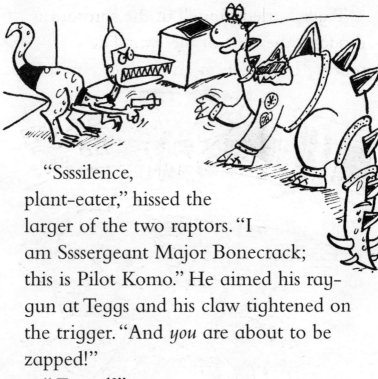

"Ssssilence,
plant-eater," hissed the
larger of the two raptors. "I
am Ssssergeant Major Bonecrack;
this is Pilot Komo." He aimed his ray-
gun at Teggs and his claw tightened on
the trigger. "And *you* are about to be
zapped!"

"*Zapped?*"

Teggs and his fellow cadets jumped as
the frozen figure in the captain's chair
burst into life. "*I'LL SHOW YOU
ZAPPED!*" the torosaurus bellowed,
pulling an identical ray-gun from her
pocket. She blasted Pilot Komo in the
chest and he fell over with a squawk –
just as Bonecrack fired back at her.

Teggs hurled himself at the torosaurus, dragging her out of the way. The searing blast blew up a bank of controls.

But the raptor didn't get a chance to fire again. Dutch reared up and punched him with both fists. Bonecrack slammed into the wall and slid down in a senseless heap.

Netta checked both raptors. "They're wearing armour – they're not badly hurt."

"Give me those guns," said the torosaurus, snatching the weapons from the carnivores' claws.

"Who are you?" Damona demanded, as she helped Teggs to his feet.

"I'm Captain Liress, kid," the torosaurus informed her. "But who in space are you?"

"They are very promising astrosaur cadets," said Erick, appearing in the doorway with a startled Blink and Splatt. "I am their flight instructor, Colonel Erick, at your service. We were exploring upstairs when we heard the explosion and came running."

"Everything's under control, Colonel," said Liress. "Your cadets did good."

Erick saluted. "May I present Teggs, Dutch, Damona, Netta, Blink and Splatt. We found your ship by accident when we crash-landed close by."

Splatt eyed the two sleeping raptors nervously. "How did they get on board?"

"I don't know." Liress sighed. "I don't even remember how *I* got here. Where *is* here, anyway? How's the war going?"

49

Blink blinked. "Er, we won it – sixty years ago!"

Liress stared at him in amazement. "*What?*"

"It's true," Erick assured her.

The torosaurus scratched her three-horned head. "I . . . I must have lost my memory!"

"Probably a side-effect of being on ice for sixty years," Blink mused, cradling his injured wing. "You haven't aged a day – but your memories are still frozen!"

"I'm sure they'll soon come back," said Teggs kindly.

But Liress was looking sharply at Netta. "Hey, kid, that bracelet you're wearing . . . it reminds me of something."

"I found it in the lab on Level One," said Netta, holding out her wrist. "I was only keeping it safe till we found the owner, honest. Is it yours?"

"No idea," Liress admitted. "You can keep it, kid. My mind's a total blank. Aside from my name and rank, I can't tell you a thing."

"And now *we* can't tell the outside world that we're stuck down here." Dutch turned from the wrecked control panel to look glumly at Erick. "That explosion you heard was a raptor ray-blast – he blew up the communications system!"

"Oh, no," groaned Blink.

Teggs rounded on the raptors as they started to stir. "Komo is a pilot, so he must have come in some kind of spaceship. Perhaps we can signal from there."

"What ship?" Pilot Komo looked blank. "I don't remember."

"Nor do I," said Bonecrack. "And even if I did, why would I tell you?"

"Um, maybe 'cos we're stuck with no food, in freezing tunnels, a mile under the ground, with a giant hairy spider after us?" Dutch suggested.

The raptors scowled, but Liress stared into space as if chasing a memory. "Giant spider? That rings a bell."

Teggs frowned. "You mean that monster was skulking around sixty years ago?"

"I bet it's still waiting for us outside!" said Damona.

Suddenly, they heard a loud clang from the corridor.

Blink hopped through the door to take a look – then dashed back inside, blinking so hard he almost started a whirlwind. "The giant spider *isn't* waiting for us outside," he announced. "It's got *inside* – and it's coming our way!"

Even as he spoke, the huge hairy monster loomed up in the doorway, its dark mouth twitching and its red eyes burning like coals . . .

Chapter Six

TUNNEL TROUBLE

Teggs, Damona, Blink and Dutch stood rooted to the spot in horror. Splatt squealed and jumped into Netta's arms, and *she* jumped with Splatt into Erick's arms – squashing him flat.

The raptors clutched on to each other, trembling with fright. "Shoot it, sssomebody!" rasped Bonecrack.

Liress fired her ray-gun, but the spider barely seemed to notice. Its fiery gaze had settled on Netta. She backed away quickly – but the monster lumbered towards her, striding straight over Splatt as it did so.

"Help!" cried Netta. "It's after me!"

Teggs bravely galloped over and shoved Netta clear with his tail. He squared up to the spider – but it ignored him completely and went after Netta again!

"We're off!" shouted Bonecrack, as he and the pilot fled through the open door.

"After them!" Liress yelled. "Now that thing's not blocking the doorway – everyone out!"

Damona grabbed Netta and pulled her away. Teggs, Dutch and Blink charged after them. Super-speedy Splatt outran them all – until he realized he didn't know where he was going and quickly skidded to a stop! Erick and Liress sprinted from the control room

and closed the door behind them,
trapping the spider inside. It roared and
beat its legs against the thick metal.

"That door won't hold for long," said
Erick grimly. "Liress, did you have any
crew on board this ship?"

Liress shook her head. "I always work
alone – my missions are too secret to
share with anyone else." She frowned.
"The emergency exit is on the level
below. I think I might know my way
round those tunnels you spoke of . . ."

Blink looked hopeful. "Perhaps you can lead us all to the surface?"

"Even if she can't, we might find the raptor ship on our way," said Damona.

"I want to find those raptors, too," Liress declared. "Come on!"

She led the group down the steps to Level One, then through a maze of dimly lit corridors. Soon they reached the emergency exit – and found the doors wide open.

"The raptors got away," said Erick bitterly.

Freezing cold air blew in from outside, chilling Teggs to the tips of his tail-spikes. But to his surprise, the tunnel ahead of them was lit with a smoky orange glow. The light came from several flaming torches placed in holders on the jagged rock walls.

"Everlasting torches!" Blink declared. "I've read about these – very handy in a power cut. The DSS used them in wartime before they invented the everlasting battery."

"Thanks for the lecture, beak-brain!" said Damona. "But how did they get here?"

"I must have put them up — sixty years ago." Liress strode outside and pulled free the nearest torch. "I guess I used this tunnel a lot!"

"Well," said Erick, helping himself to a torch and passing another to Teggs. "Now we can see, let's go after those raptors."

Liress led the way. Teggs and his friends followed her. Bringing up the rear, Erick closed the spaceship's exit before trailing after the others into the flickering, smoky shadows.

Netta fiddled nervously with her borrowed bracelet. "Ever have the feeling you're being watched?"

"Yes," Blink whispered. "Right now!"

"Shhh," said Splatt, gesturing for everyone to stop. "I think I heard something."

"Just your imagination," said Liress, holding up her torch. "There's nothing in front of us."

Erick waved his own torch back the way they'd come. "And nothing behind us."

Then Teggs heard a scuttling noise overhead. Heart pounding, he held up his own torch . . .

And saw *two* giant spiders clinging to the rocky ceiling above them!

Splatt shrieked, and Netta gasped as one of the monsters reached down and grabbed her.

"Get your hairy legs off my friend!" shouted Damona, striking the spider with her horns. It flicked her aside and sent her crashing into Erick.

Liress fired her ray-gun again, but then the other spider dropped to the ground – almost squashing Teggs, Blink and Dutch as it did so – and knocked both the torch and the weapon from her grip.

"Help!" shouted Netta as the two spiders dragged her away.

"What do those things want with her?" wailed Splatt.

"We must follow them," said Liress, her eyes growing wider. "I – I've just remembered the secret of the spiders!"

Teggs stared at her. "What is it?"

"Forget the talk," snarled Damona. "Try some action!" She charged at the nearest spider, but it blocked her attack with its back legs and pushed her away.

"Ooof!" she gasped as she staggered into Dutch.

"Argh!" Dutch slipped backwards and sat on Blink.

"Eeek!" yelped Blink, as the force of Dutch's landing sent him skidding along the icy ground on his tummy. The pair of them crashed straight into Teggs – "*Wughh!*" – and knocked him off his feet.

Teggs dropped his torch as all three Daring Dinos slid helplessly into a side-

tunnel – which dipped suddenly and
sharply like a toboggan run!

"Guys!" yelled Erick helplessly, as
Teggs, Blink and Dutch vanished from
sight.

"Hang onto something!" cried Teggs,
clawing desperately at the smooth

slippery ice as they picked up speed.

"My wing," Blink gasped. "Can't get a grip . . ."

"Look out, dudes!" Dutch shouted as they whizzed faster and faster down the ice slide. "I think we're about to run out of—*Whoaaaaa!*"

Suddenly, the ground fell away. Terrified, the three friends tumbled helplessly through empty space . . .

Chapter Seven

LAIR OF DANGER

Down the Daring Dinos fell, spinning and somersaulting. Teggs opened his mouth to yell . . .

"Look out!" came a cold, rasping voice from somewhere beneath him. "You sssssstupid ssssssssstego—"

Scrunch! Slammm! Whudd!

Teggs, Dutch and Blink struck something in the darkness. They hit it so hard that the breath was thumped from their bodies. But whatever had stopped their fall now rocked wildly beneath them. It felt to Teggs like he'd landed on a squashy, scaly trampoline.

Then he heard a groan of pain up

close in his ear!

"Blink? Dutch?" Teggs scratched his head. "I think I've landed right on top of Pilot Komo!"

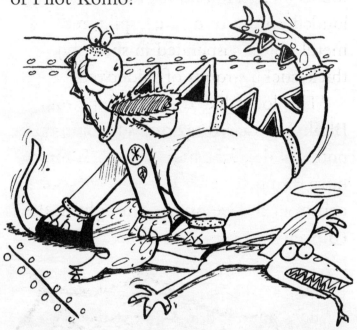

"The raptors must have fallen down the same tunnel as we did when they ran away," Blink realized.

"I wish I'd landed on Bonecrack's belly instead of on my butt," groaned Dutch. "The ground feels like it's metal – how come it's rocking?"

Teggs carefully stepped away from Komo's body, and as his eyes adjusted to the feeble light he gasped in amazement. He and his friends had landed on top of a large, spiky red metal object suspended in space by thick, sticky strands of spiderweb.

"This looks like a raptor ship," said Blink. He looked up, and saw a faint patch of daylight high above. "It must have dropped down into this colossal chasm in the ice and got caught in the cobweb!"

"A web strong enough to stop a *spaceship*?" Teggs helped Dutch to his feet. "That's crazy!"

"We could not believe it either," came a grating voice close by. "But it's true!"

Teggs spun around and saw Sergeant Major Bonecrack's ugly head sticking out of a hatch in the spaceship roof.

"I remember now, you ssssee," hissed the raptor. "We were on a vital war mission to find and destroy Captain Liress's ssssecret experiments. But our ship got caught in this web and we were taken prisoner . . ." Suddenly, he grabbed the dazed Komo and dragged him through the hatch. "Luckily, my pilot prepared our escape before you ssssquashed him.

As ssssoon as our power cells are recharged, we will be free – free to complete our mission and destroy you all!" With that, he ducked down through the hatch and slammed the cover behind him.

"Looks like it's up to the Daring Dinos to stop him, dudes," said Dutch, holding out his hand. "We must break in and pull him back out. Do we dare?"

Teggs and Blink put their hands on his. "WE DARE!"

But suddenly, Blink froze. "Unfortunately," he twittered, "I think *they* might have other ideas!"

Teggs and Dutch turned to find six pairs of glowing red eyes staring out of the darkness on either side of them.

"Of course," Teggs realized grimly. "This web bridges the split in the ice between two tunnels. That must be why the spiders chose this spot to spin it – so they can cross from one side to the other."

Before he could say another word, the monsters spilled out from the tunnels and grabbed them with their thick, hairy legs. The cadets struggled to escape, but it was no good.

"Where are they taking us?" Blink cried.

"Dunno," Dutch gasped, as the spiders hauled them away into a gloomy passageway lit by more of the everlasting torches. "But I bet it's not for a pizza and a movie!"

Teggs tried to stay calm while he was
dragged through a maze of narrow, icy
tunnels. Then, as they rounded a slippery
corner, he saw an eerie red glow
coming from the mouth of a cave up
ahead. Seconds later, with a thrill of
terror, Teggs realized the light was

coming from the eyes of *hundreds* of giant spiders! The creatures sat squashed up together in an enormous cavern, their huge hairy bodies twitching and quivering.

Teggs sensed that he and his friends had reached the very heart of the spiders' lair . . .

Chapter Eight

SECRET OF THE SPIDERS

"Guys!" came a familiar female cry from the middle of the cave. "I'm *so* glad you're all right!"

Teggs stopped struggling and swapped startled looks with Dutch and Blink. "*Netta?*"

"Spiders – thank you for finding my friends," she said. "Now put them down and let them approach!"

Suddenly, the sea of spiders parted to reveal the pink ankylosaur perched on a rocky outcrop in the middle of the cave, holding up one hand. Damona, Splatt, Captain Liress and Colonel Erick were huddled around her.

Blink looked bewildered as his spider gently set him down. "Netta, they're doing as you say!"

"Of course," she said. "I told them to find you and bring you back here."

Teggs and Dutch also found themselves being released. The three cadets edged carefully through the ranks of spiders to rejoin their friends. Erick opened his mouth to speak, but Damona, as usual, got there first.

"The spiders aren't really bad at all!" she said breathlessly. "They're actually quite nice once you get used to them.

They only wanted Netta because of that bracelet she found!"

"It's a top-secret control device I was working on," Liress explained. "It turns dinosaur speech into spider mind-commands."

"So whoever wears it controls the giant spiders!" added Splatt. "You see, they don't want to hurt us at all. They were only after instructions."

"I felt that we were being steered towards Liress's ship," Teggs recalled. "The

spiders *wanted* us to find that bracelet."

Blink nodded. "And when Netta put it on, she must have activated it – and so the spiders came running!"

"I trained them well," said Liress. "I found the spiders on an expedition to Mygos, a dying world, and brought them here because I believed they could help us win the war; their webs are so strong they can even stop spaceships in their tracks."

"Safely capturing both the crew and

their craft without using weapons," Erick marvelled. "Brilliant!"

"I used the bracelet to tell the spiders where to spin their webs," Liress went on. "I knew enemy raptors would come looking for my underground base, so I left web-nets all around to catch them."

"They really work," said Blink. "When we fell down that slippery tunnel, we found Sergeant Major Bonecrack's ship caught in one."

"Luckily, it caught us, too!" Dutch added.

Liress nodded. "Capturing Bonecrack's craft was my first successful web-net test. The spiders dragged the raptors back to my mega-jet, and I was about to report to DSS HQ when the engines started an avalanche."

"Your ship was buried," Teggs realized. "And as the years passed, the spiders took over the tunnels while you and the raptors stayed frozen – until Erick thawed you out."

"Pity Bonecrack and Komo thawed out first and caught me and Netta," said Damona darkly.

"That's a point," said Dutch. "Those scaly scumbags are back in their ship, getting ready to blow us all up!"

"Hah!" Liress scoffed. "Bonecrack's Doom-Bringer battlecraft could never break free of that web."

"Doom-Bringer, you say?" Erick grabbed hold of her urgently. "Was it a mark one or mark two?"

Liress frowned. "I didn't know there even *was* a mark two!"

"It was brought into action at the end of Raptor War Ten," Erick explained. "The mark twos were fitted with a secret assault shuttle inside, ready to burst out if the Doom-Bringer was hit so that the crew could carry on fighting!"

"Bonecrack *said* Komo had prepared their escape," Blink recalled with a squawk of alarm.

Teggs nodded. "He must have been making sure the shuttle wouldn't get tangled up in the web around the main ship."

"I'll send the spiders to get them," Netta declared.

Erick shook his head. "Raptor assault shuttles came with a powerful energy shield. Not even the spiders could dent it."

"But they *could* weave a web above

the shuttle to
catch it when
Bonecrack
tries to leave,"
said Blink.

Dutch
beamed.
"Sweet plan, dude!"

"It will take time
to spin a web that
tough," warned Liress.

"Then you'd better get started." Netta
handed her the bracelet. "This is yours,
Captain Liress – get those spiders on the
case!"

"But first, I need one to carry me to
the surface," said Erick. "I must warn
Commander Gruff to alert the
academy's air defences – so if those
raptors *do* escape, they won't get much
further."

"The way out will be slippery and
unsafe," Liress warned him.

"Then it sounds like a job for Damona's Darlings," said Damona, and Splatt and Netta agreed. "There's three of us. We can watch out for each other."

"She's right, sir," said Teggs.

Damona fluttered her eyelashes. "Aren't I always?"

Erick sighed. "Very well."

Liress put on the bracelet, shut her eyes and pointed to three of the giant spiders. "Take my friends to the surface as quickly and carefully as you can!"

The spiders crouched down so
Damona, Netta and Splatt could climb
on board. Then they whisked the
dinosaurs out of the cavern at incredible
speed.

"Good luck, dudes!" called Dutch, and Teggs and Blink whooped and clapped.

"See you soon!" Damona yelled back.

"Right," said Liress. "Let's check out that chasm so we know which bit to web up."

But as she led the way out of the spiders' cavern, Teggs suddenly felt the ground tremble beneath his feet.

"What's that?" Blink twittered. "An earthquake?"

"Feels more like engine vibrations," said Erick grimly. "The raptors must have started up their assault shuttle. They're getting ready for take-off!"

Chapter Nine

HANGING BY A THREAD

"Quickly," said Captain Liress, leaping on the back of the nearest giant spider. "Eight legs can move quicker than two or four!" She touched her bracelet. "Spiders, you will look after my friends and do whatever they ask."

The creatures bowed down.

"How long before the raptors blast off, Colonel?" asked Teggs, swinging himself onto a broad hairy back.

"After sixty years, the engines will take a while to warm up . . ." Erick climbed onto his own giant spider and shrugged. "About an hour, I'd say – or maybe less."

Liress looked worried. "We need more time!"

"Then we must slow Bonecrack down," said Dutch, balancing on a spider with Blink. "We could bring down an avalanche on top of the raptor ship!" Teggs suggested.

Erick nodded. "The shuttle's energy shield will soon melt the snow and ice – but it might just buy the spiders the time they need."

Liress clapped Teggs on the back. "Smart thinking, kid. Now, follow me, all of you!"

Her spider shot off at remarkable

speed. Teggs gasped as his own spider
zoomed after her, with Erick, Dutch and
Blink close behind on their own eight-
legged steeds.

The monsters skittered and skidded
through the dark, icy tunnels, their eyes
lighting the way like crimson
headlamps. And as they raced along,
Teggs could feel the vibrations in the
ground getting gradually stronger.

The minutes passed in a blur.
Suddenly, they reached the mouth of a
tunnel overlooking the raptor Doom-
Bringer battlecraft. A large split had

appeared in the frozen metal, and Teggs could see the pointed tip of a smaller ship inside.

"There's the assault shuttle," breathed Erick. "All set to burst out."

"There are some tunnels that come out a few hundred metres higher up," said Liress, steering her spider away. "I'll get my hairy friends to whip up a web-net across the chasm right now."

Teggs turned to the other cadets, "Meanwhile, it's time for a home-made avalanche . . ." He held out his hand. "Do we dare?"

Blink and Dutch slapped their hands
down on his, and even Erick joined in.
"WE DARE!"

Racing against time in the red glare
of the spiders' eyes, the dinosaurs went
to work.

Teggs swung his
spiky tail like a
pickaxe,
splintering
chunks of
ice from
the floor.

Dutch checked out cracks high up in the tunnel walls, then balanced Blink on his head. The dino-bird used his beak as a chisel to peck at the cracks, prising more ice away. As the minutes passed by they worked harder and harder, barely saying a word, pushing themselves to the limit. Erick piled up the icy rubble and the spiders helped shove it to the edge of the chasm ready to be hurled down over the raptor ship.

But suddenly the steady thrum of the shuttle's engines changed pitch, growing higher and louder. Teggs fell to his knees as the tunnel began to shake.

"Sounds like Bonecrack's ready to go!" Erick cried.

"He mustn't!" panted Blink. "We haven't got enough rubble yet!"

Teggs stared down helplessly as the shuttle rose slowly out of its hiding place in the shell of the Doom-Bringer battlecraft. The vibrations tore through the tunnel and it was hard to stay standing.

"It's now or never!" shouted Erick. He heaved at the huge pile of boulders and Teggs, Dutch and Blink joined in, pushing numbly at the ice with aching arms.

"It's starting to go!" Teggs yelled. "One more shove . . ." But as the teetering ice pile finally gave way, he slipped and lost his balance – and went over the edge with the avalanche!

"Dude!" Dutch yelled helplessly.

Teggs plummeted towards the ship below in a hail of boulders. The assault shuttle's energy shield activated, buzzing and sizzling as it turned the chunks of ice to slush. Teggs closed his eyes . . .

But before he could hit the shield, thick, hairy legs locked around his waist and he was jerked back up into the air like a bungee-jumper. Teggs opened his eyes in amazement. One of the giant spiders had leaped after him to save his life – and now the two of them were dangling from the ledge above by a thin strand of web!

"Thank goodness!" cried Blink, while Dutch and Erick wiped their brows. "Liress told the spiders to look after us – I'm just glad they listened!"

"But the avalanche has failed," said Erick gravely. "It was too small – the raptors' shields burned it off in seconds."

Suddenly, a rasping voice, colder than the ice all around, rang out over the engines' building growl. It was Bonecrack. "Your pathetic attempt to sssstop us has failed," he sneered over the shuttle's loudspeakers. "We will now take off and destroy you . . ."

Teggs craned his neck to check the web-net above. Strands hung across the chasm like a silky hammock.

Could they stop a spaceship? "Let's get up there and help!" he told his spider.

Shooting out another sticky thread the spider launched itself, with Teggs, across the chasm heading for the nearest tunnel on the far side. But as it did so, the assault shuttle suddenly shot up and its tail-fins snagged on the web-strand.

"Whoa!" gasped Teggs as he and the spider were yanked through the air at incredible speed, and then dragged behind the small spaceship like tin cans tied to the back of a car. Teggs choked on thick clouds of exhaust and felt his tough skin prickling in the heat of the shuttle's rockets . . .

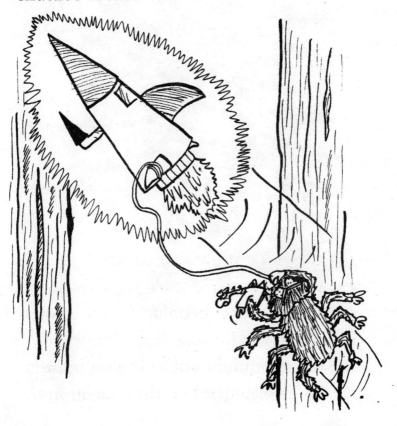

Then – *KA-BOINNNG!* The raptor-craft hit Liress's chasm-blocking cobweb head on. Its energy shield glowed electric blue as it tried to push on through, with Teggs and the spider still hanging on underneath. The web-net crackled and smoked as the straining shuttle stretched it further and further . . .

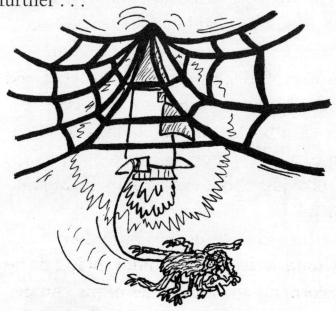

"It's no good," Teggs gasped as the whine of engines reached a deafening shriek. "Bonecrack's going to break free!"

Chapter Ten

WAR'S END

The web-net was beginning to tear. Bonecrack's mad laughter echoed out over the din of the engines. And the strand of sticky web that held Teggs and his spider was starting to smoulder . . .

"If it breaks, the fall might kill me . . ." Teggs gave a crooked smile. "Like just about everything else around here!"

But suddenly, as if to prove him wrong, at least thirty giant spiders came swarming down the sides of the chasm! Spinning thick cushions of cobweb to protect them from the energy field, more and more of them hurled themselves onto the assault shuttle as it tried to force its way upwards. Soon the web-net was a seething mass of spiders, and the raptor-ship was lost from view.

"Fantastic!" cheered Teggs as still more spiders piled on. "They're using their bodies as well as their webs to block the shuttle's path!"

Finally, with a throaty bang, the assault craft's straining engines exploded. The energy shield faded and died, and the shuttle was left hanging uselessly in a mass of smoking web.

The spider carrying Teggs swiftly scaled its smoking web-strand and placed him safely on its back. Far below, through the smoke and gloom, Teggs could see Dutch, Blink and Erick perched on the ledge, cheering and waving.

Then, Liress came out onto the smouldering web-net on the back of another spider.

Teggs saluted her. "Good work, Captain."

"Thanks, kid!" Liress winked at him. "Now, spiders – get those raptors!"

Her hairy servants tore apart the assault shuttle to reveal Bonecrack and Komo fuming inside. "Plant-eating ssssscum!" snarled the sergeant major.

Liress held out her arm. "Talk to the
hand, losers!" she said, before the spiders
imprisoned the carnivores in a thick
web cocoon.

"Congratulations, Captain Liress,"
came a booming, amplified voice from
high above. "You too, cadets."

Teggs gasped and jumped down from
his spider. "That sounds like
Commander Gruff!"

Looking skyward, he saw two astro-copters buzzing down through the chasm towards them. Gruff was piloting the bigger one, and Teggs smiled to see Damona steering the smaller astro-copter, with Splatt and Netta waving madly from the back seats.

"Told you I was a cool pilot!" Damona called.

But Teggs hardly heard her over the victory whoops of Dutch, Blink and Erick as they rushed out onto the web-net to celebrate with hugs and dancing. Liress climbed off her spider and joined in – once she'd commanded three spiders to spin a webby platform for the astro-copters to land on.

After making a perfect landing, Damona jumped out of the 'copter with Netta and Splatt. "The spiders were brilliant," she said, her eyes shining. "They led us all the way out and straight to one of Commander Gruff's search patrols."

Gruff himself emerged from his giant astro-copter. "I certainly didn't expect to find a missing war hero, two raptor criminals and a load of giant alien spiders down here with you!" He picked up Bonecrack and Komo with his tail and chucked them in the back of the 'copter. "Those two did terrible things during the war. They will go to space prison for a long, long time."

"Good riddance!" shouted Netta.

Teggs breathed a sigh of relief. "It seems that Raptor War Ten is finally over."

"Thanks to Captain Liress," said Erick.

"No," said Liress. "Thanks to my brave, loyal spiders. I trained them to help us against the raptors, and they waited sixty years for their chance. But now the war has ended, I think they deserve a special reward . . ."

Gruff smiled and nodded. "Their freedom."

Liress wiped a tear from her eyes, pulled off her control bracelet and handed it to Teggs. "Here, kid. You do it."

Taking a deep breath, Teggs squashed
the bracelet into a metal ball. He tossed
it to Blink, who headed it to Dutch,
who used his tail to whack the
crumpled control device far into the
distance. Set free at last, the spiders
bowed their heads to Liress one last
time, then crawled happily back to their
cobwebby homes in the ice tunnels.

"You deserve a reward too, Captain Liress." Gruff smiled. "We're having a big reunion party here today to celebrate the end of the war."

"You'll get to see all your old friends!" Teggs told her.

"*Old* is right." Liress chuckled.

"And in front of them all, you'll receive a special medal," Gruff went on.

"Much obliged, Commander." Liress saluted. "But the best reward would be a new job in the Dinosaur Space Service – once I've caught up on everything I've missed over the last sixty years!"

"It's yours," Gruff told her.

Dutch beamed. "This is going to be the wildest celebration ever!"

"And all you cadets will be guests of honour," Gruff declared. "I'm going to give *you* each a medal too."

"Wow!" Teggs gasped. "Thanks, sir!"

"Cool!" yelled Splatt. "Damona, you should crash expensive DSS spacecraft more often!"

"He's joking," Blink added hastily.

"And speaking of spacecraft," said Erick, "Liress's lovely old mega-jet still needs restoring. I'll give extra flying lessons to anyone who helps me dig it out." He looked round. "Any volunteers?"

"Me! Me!" Teggs and Dutch shouted over the enthusiastic cries of the other

cadets, jumping up and down with their
hands up.

"You can start tomorrow," Gruff told
them all. "In the meantime, you've got a
party to enjoy – and that's an order!"

The cadets grinned and saluted. "Yes,
sir!"

Erick followed Damona, Splatt and
Netta to their 'copter while Teggs, Dutch,
Blink and Liress joined Gruff and the
raptors in his. As they took off, Teggs
glimpsed a hairy leg waving goodbye
from the mouth of a tunnel.

"The spiders are free and happy now," Liress murmured.

Teggs smiled. "And thanks to them, so are we!"

Then the gloom of the chasm gave way to the brilliant blue skies of Astro Prime.

Safe at last, Teggs, Blink and Dutch settled back and grinned, thinking over their amazing escapades – and dreaming of the incredible adventures still to come.

THE END